MOUSE TRAIL

By Mary Octavia Davis

Steck-Vaughn Company   Austin, Texas

For
my great nieces and nephews

Helen Irene Davis
Francis Marion Davis III
Matthew Stephen Davis
Robert Rothe Davis
Mary Patricia Davis
John Reinhart Davis

and
in memory of

Elizabeth Ann Davis

Little Mouse was excited.
He had learned all his numbers.
Today he could go into the Big Swamp
all
by
himself.

3

Little Mouse's mother brushed his golden coat.
She told him all the things he should watch for.
"Stay on the mouse trails," she warned him.
"Follow the numbers."
Little Mouse could not hold still.
"Hurry, Mother, hurry!   I want to GO."

Little Mouse dashed out the door.
Then he stopped and waved to his mother.
"Good-by, Mother."
"Good-by, Little Mouse," she called.
"Be careful. Look and listen—and
remember
your
numbers!"

A hungry shrew was catching bugs.
She saw Little Mouse coming.
   "Hum," she said. "Just what I want
   for my dinner—a fat little mouse."
Then she got ready to catch him.

The spider spinning his web saw her.
He dropped his thread.
"Look out, Little Mouse!" he called.
"SHREW!"
Little Mouse jumped into a tall flower.
The shrew could not find him.
"Thank you for the warning,"
said Little Mouse.
Then he went on down the mouse trail.

A big blue snake was hunting frogs.
He saw Little Mouse coming.

"Hum," he said. "Just what I want
for my dinner—a fat little mouse."
Then he got ready to catch him.

Mouse Trail Route 2

The chameleon on a twig saw him.
    "Look out, Little Mouse!" he
    called.
        "BLUE SNAKE!"
Little Mouse swung to the top of a bush.
The snake could not find him.
    "Thank you for the warning," said
    Little Mouse.
Then he went on down the mouse trail.

A big bobcat was looking for squirrels.
He saw Little Mouse coming.

"Hum," he said. "Just what I want for
my dinner—a fat little mouse."

Then he got ready to catch him.

The squirrel hiding an
acorn saw him.
He dropped his acorn.
    "Look out, Little Mouse!"
    he called.
            "BOBCAT!"
Little Mouse ran through a tunnel.
The bobcat could not find him.
    "Thank you for the warning," said
    Little Mouse.
Then he went on down the mouse trail.

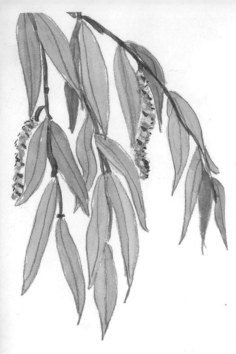

A weasel was sunning himself
by some rocks.
He slyly pretended to be asleep.
He heard Little Mouse coming.
  "Hum," he said. "Just what
  I want for my dinner—a fat
  little mouse."
Then he got ready to catch him.

Danger!
Use This
← Trail.

A wood duck sitting on her nest saw him.
She stuck her head out of the tree hole.
    "Look out, Little Mouse!" she called.
        "WEASEL!"
Little Mouse ran behind the rocks.
The weasel could not find him.
    "Thank you for the warning,"
    said Little Mouse.
Then he went on down the mouse trail.

"Oh," said Little
Mouse, "this Big
Swamp is SCARY!"
He looked all around.
He listened.
Then he darted into
the open.
A hawk saw him.
  "Hum," he said.
  "Just what I want
  for my dinner—a
  fat little mouse."
Then he got ready to
catch him.

The woodpecker pecking on a tree
saw him.
He stopped his pecking.
     "Look out, Little Mouse!" he called.
         "HAWK!"
Little Mouse ran into a hole in the tree.
The hawk could not find him.
     "Thank you for the warning," said
     Little Mouse.
Then he went on down the mouse trail.

Hole
Inn

Mouse
Trail
Route 6

Some herons were fishing for minnows
in the shallow water.
One of them saw Little Mouse coming.
 "Hum," he said. "Just what I want
 for my dinner—a fat little mouse."
Then he got ready to catch him.

Mouse
Trail
Route 7

Muskrat
Tunnel

DUTZ

The kingfisher, who was fishing too, saw him.
He dropped his fish.
    "Look out, Little Mouse!" he called.
        "HERON!"
Little Mouse ran into a pile of sticks.
The heron could not find him.
    "Thank you for the warning,"
    said Little Mouse.
Then he went on down the mouse trail—
        but now he was being
        very careful.

Mouse
Trail
Route 8

A sleek otter was sliding down his mud slide.
He saw Little Mouse coming.

"Hum," he said. "Just what I want for
my dinner—a fat little mouse."

Then he got ready to catch him.

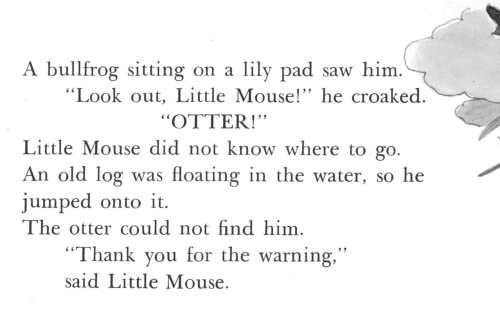

A bullfrog sitting on a lily pad saw him.
"Look out, Little Mouse!" he croaked.
"OTTER!"
Little Mouse did not know where to go.
An old log was floating in the water, so he
jumped onto it.
The otter could not find him.
"Thank you for the warning,"
said Little Mouse.

Little Mouse was very tired.
He curled up on the log and went to sleep.
He did not notice that the log was moving
slowly,
slowly.
The log did not make a sound as it moved
through the water.

A blackbird perched on a reed
saw Little Mouse sleeping.
He saw the log moving.
    "Wake up, Little Mouse, wake up!" he called.
        "ALLIGATOR!"
Little Mouse woke up.
    "Thank you for the warning,"
    said Little Mouse.
He looked around for the alligator.
    "Oh, oh! I'm moving! I'm
    ON
    THE
    ALLIGATOR!"

Little Mouse ran up and down the
alligator.

What could he do?

Where could he go?

All around was water.

Then the alligator slowly lifted his
long, long tail
out of the water.

Little Mouse ran to the tip of the tail.

Suddenly the long, long tail gave a
        FLIP-FLOP.
Up in the air went Little Mouse.
    "Where am I going?" he cried.
    "Oh,
        Oh,
        Oh!"

Mouse
Trail
Route II

23

SPLASH!

He landed in the shallow water.

He was very wet when he waded out.

He looked around until he found the mouse trail.

Then something went

"Crack, CRACK, BOOM!"

The sky darkened.

Little Mouse wanted to go home—

but the sign had no number to help him.

Little Mouse ran
        and ran
        and ran.
He came to another sign,
but there was no number on it either.
        Little Mouse was lost.
Still, he remembered to stay on the mouse trail.

On and on ran Little Mouse.
Ahead were the crossroads.
The trails had many signs,
but no numbers.
"I'm lost.
I want to go home," cried
Little Mouse.
Then he saw Grandfather Muskrat.

"Help me, Grandfather Muskrat," begged
Little Mouse.
He pointed to the darkening sky.
    "Look! It's going to rain, and I'm lost
    because the signs do not have any numbers."
Then Little Mouse began to cry.
    "How can I get home?"

"Don't cry, Little Mouse," said
Grandfather Muskrat kindly.
"Don't you know what to do?
    Whenever you roam,
    To find the way home,
    As any mouse knows,
    Just follow your nose!"

"Crack, CRACK, BOOM!"
A big drop of rain fell.
Then another!
And another!
Away went the muskrat.
Away went Little Mouse.
He did not see the sun trying to peep out.
Little Mouse was too busy looking for a sign
with
a number.

Little Mouse ran on and on.
Everywhere he looked he saw something
        EYEING him.
They all had their mouths wide open
to eat him.
He wished he could find his mother.

High Bridge

Dead End

Suddenly he saw Little Fawn.
"Help me. I'm lost," said
Little Mouse tearfully.
Little Fawn shook her head.
"You are not lost.
Your home is just around the bend.
Your mother is looking for you."
Little Mouse thanked her and hurried on.
Soon he came to a sign that said "Route 1."
He followed the trail around the bend—
and there was his mother.